Sid the Sheep

Written by Teresa Heapy

Illustrated by Carolina Delavy Chagas

Collins

Sid the sheep had tight curls.

His hair got bigger and bigger.

It got tighter and tighter.

Ow!

The farmer cut off the hair.

Now Sid needed a hat.

13

Sid the sheep

 After reading

Letters and Sounds: Phase 3

Word count: 58

Focus phonemes: /ee/ /igh/ /oo/ /oo/ /ur/ /ow/ /ear/ /air/ /er/ /ar/

Common exception words: the, my, and, no, you

Curriculum links: Understanding the world

Early learning goals: Reading: read and understand simple sentences; use phonic knowledge to decode regular words and read them aloud accurately; read some common irregular words

Developing fluency

- Your child may enjoy hearing you read the book.
- Take turns to read a page, but encourage your child to read all the speech bubbles. Remind them to think about how the characters are feeling and to look out for the exclamation marks and question mark so that they can read expressively.

Phonic practice

- Focus on the words with long vowels which are made up of three letters. Challenge your child to find words with these sounds and spellings:

  /igh/ (*tight, tighter*)   /air/ (*hair*)   /ear/ (*shear, dear*)

- Challenge your child to think of a word that has the same spelling, and perhaps rhymes with each of these: **tight**, **hair**, **dear**. (e.g. *light, might*; *fair, lair*; *fear, tear*)

Extending vocabulary

- Read the text on page 7. Ask: What does Sid need? Together say: *He needs a shear.*
- Read the text on page 12 and discuss how the "-ed" shows that Sid needed a hat in the past, not now. Ask: What did Sid need? Together say: *He needed a hat.*
- You could take turns to ask and answer: What do you need today? (*I need …*) What did you need yesterday? (*I needed …*)